D0255039

AGE9753-1

The Fairfield Friends Devotional Adventures

Firecracker Power and Other Stories
The Lightning Escape and Other Stories
Blaze on Rocky Ridge and Other Stories

9708

NANCY SPECK

A FAIRFIELD FRIENDS DEVOTIONAL ADVENTURE

BLAZE ON ROCKY RIDGE

And
OTHER STORIES

BETHANY HOUSE PUBLISHERS
MINNEAPOLIS, MINNESOTA 55438

Blaze on Rocky Ridge
Copyright © 1997
Nancy Speck

Cover illustration by Neverne Covington
Text illustrations by Joe Nordstrom

Published by Bethany House Publishers
A Ministry of Bethany Fellowship, Inc.
11300 Hampshire Avenue South
Minneapolis, Minnesota 55438

Printed in the United States of America.

Library of Congress Cataloging-in-Publication Data

CIP Data applied for

ISBN 0–7642–2006–3   CIP

CL 8/98

To my favorite high school English teacher
and elementary principal
(a.k.a. Mom and Dad)

NANCY SPECK is a free-lance writer and home-maker who has published numerous articles, stories, and poems. Her background in creative writing and social work gives her unique insight into the importance and challenge of teaching children Christian character traits at an early age. Nancy and her husband, Brian, have two elementary-age daughters and make their home in Pennsylvania.

Contents

Cameron Parker

Cameron is very smart in math and science and is in third grade at a private school, Foster Academy. He lives with his parents, older brother, Philip, and younger sister, Justine.

Ceely Coleman

Ceely, short for Cecilia, is hardworking and serious. She is in fourth grade at Morgandale Christian School, plays field hockey, and has a black cat named Snowball.

Hutch Coleman

Hutch, short for Hutchinson, is Ceely's younger brother. He's a second grader at Morgandale Christian School and is the class clown.

# of Fairfield Court

Min Hing

Min, a third-grade student at Fairfield Elementary, lives with her parents and grandmother. She's quiet and shy, takes ballet lessons, and plays the piano.

Valerie Stevens

Valerie lives with her mother and little sister, Bonnie, since her parents are divorced. Valerie, who is friendly and outspoken, is an average student in second grade at Fairfield Elementary.

Roberto Ruiz

Roberto, a fourth grader at Fairfield Elementary, has lived with his grandpop ever since his parents died. His older brother, Ramone, lives with them. Roberto plays soccer and has a dog named Freckles.

1

Waterfall Ahead!

The Fairfield Friends jumped from cars and vans and raced through the trees. They had just arrived at Laurel Lake for the yearly Fairfield Court neighborhood picnic. When the friends reached the beach, Roberto's dog, Freckles, streaked past them.

"Roberto!" yelled Grandpop from the picnic area. "Grab Freckles! He got away from me, and it's a rule that dogs must be on a leash!"

Roberto quickly dashed after the dog. But Freckles had a head start. He scampered up the beach and through the middle of another family's picnic. Potato chips flew through the air like mini Frisbees.

Finally, Roberto tackled him. He apologized to the family, then put Freckles' leash on him.

"Hey," said Roberto as he rejoined his

friends. "Look at those kids in the lake."

"But the sign at the entrance said 'No Swimming After Labor Day,' " Ceely added.

A few minutes later, the boys who had been swimming ran across the beach to the friends.

"Hi," said the taller one. "I'm Pete Stuckey, and this is my brother, Nick. We just moved into Fairfield Court."

"Oh yeah," said Roberto. "I saw the moving van last week."

"Do you know you're not supposed to be in the lake?" Cameron asked. "There are no lifeguards."

The boys shrugged. "Who cares?" answered Pete.

"You guys wanna do something or hang out?" asked Nick.

"Yeah, sure," Roberto answered.

"Let's go to the other picnic area," said Ceely, pointing.

After winding their way through some woods, they found themselves in a small grassy area.

"The picnic tables sure are close together," said Nick.

"Let's chase each other across the tops of them," Pete suggested.

"No one's allowed to walk or sit on top of

the tables," said Roberto.

"What a stupid rule," scoffed Nick. "Besides, there's no one around."

The Fairfield Friends watched Pete and Nick chase each other for a few minutes. They wanted to have fun, too. So they all stepped onto the tabletops and joined the game.

"Oww!" cried Valerie a minute later. Her foot had missed a table, and she'd scraped her shin and knee on the edge. Ceely and Min jumped down to help her. But the boys continued the chase.

"Hey!" A low, booming voice cut into the boys' laughter. "Get down from the tables." It was the park ranger. "Didn't you see the rules posted at the park entrance or on the beach?"

Roberto, Cameron, and Hutch lowered their heads in shame. Then Roberto looked up at the ranger. "We're sorry," he said.

"Yeah," muttered Hutch.

"We won't do it again," Cameron added.

The ranger nodded and turned to Nick and Pete. They stood there silently. "And I saw you two in the lake while I was at the boat dock. If you won't follow the park rules, I'll have to ask you to leave. I can also charge you a fine and not allow you back in the park."

Nick and Pete looked at their feet. But as

soon as the ranger left, they laughed.

When all eight kids arrived back at the picnic area, Mr. Coleman asked them why they looked so unhappy. The Fairfield Friends explained how Valerie hurt her leg and about the park ranger.

"Why do we have to follow all these rules?" Hutch asked.

"Many rules are made for safety reasons," explained Mr. Coleman as he poured lemonade. "But what the rules are doesn't really matter. The first five verses of chapter 13 in Romans say that 'all of you must obey the government rulers. No one rules unless God has given him the power to rule. . . . So if anyone is against the government, he is really against what God has commanded. . . . You must obey not only because you might be punished, but because you know it is the right thing to do.' "

Nick and Pete nudged each other and chuckled as they left to join their parents a few tables away.

After the six friends had finished eating, they strolled up the beach.

"Hey," said Valerie. "Why don't we go over to the boat dock and take out a couple of paddle boats."

The others agreed. But when they got to the

boathouse, they found that Nick and Pete had claimed the last boat. And the other boats wouldn't be back for an hour.

"Let's go hike Overlook Hill, then," Min suggested.

As they turned to leave, they watched Nick and Pete settle themselves into the seats on the boat.

"Here you go, kids," said the dock attendant, handing them each an orange life jacket. "Strap these on. And make sure you stay up on this part of the lake. Have fun, now."

He walked back into the boathouse. Nick and Pete threw their life vests onto the dock. The Fairfield Friends couldn't believe they were going to disobey this rule, too.

But as they walked the trail to the big hill that overlooked Laurel Lake, they forgot all about the brothers. Soon they reached the top of the hill and sat down to enjoy the view. From Overlook Hill they could see the lake, the picnic areas . . . everything.

"Look," said Hutch, pointing. "It's Nick and Pete."

"They shouldn't be that far up the lake," Ceely said.

"They're almost to the sign that says 'No Boats Past This Point,' " said Roberto.

"The dam isn't too far from there," Min added.

"And they don't have life jackets," Valerie remembered.

"Oh no!" moaned Min. "They've never been here before! They don't know that there is a dam and waterfall at the end of the lake!"

"Valerie and I will go for help," said Ceely. They started down the hill.

"But they need help *now*," said Min.

Cameron glanced around the area. He saw a volleyball net set up at the other end of the field. "C'mon," he said. "Let's get that net down."

Hutch and Roberto got to the net first. They shimmied up the poles and unhooked each side.

"To the lake!" yelled Cameron.

At the lake's edge, Cameron called to Nick and Pete. He told them the dam was up ahead and that they'd throw them the net to hold on to until help arrived.

"But the bank is too steep. We can't get down there," Min said. They peered down a fifteen-foot slope that ended at the water's edge.

Then Cameron saw the big tree that jutted out over the lake. One big limb reached over the lake even farther. "Quick, Roberto!" he

said. "Get out to the end of that branch and throw the net. I think they can reach it from there."

After crawling onto the branch, Roberto tossed the net, but it didn't quite reach. He tried again. Pete grabbed an end, but the current pulled the boat the other way. The net slipped out of his hand.

Roberto knew he had just one more chance before the boat would be past the tree. He threw the net with all his strength. Nick and Pete each caught the net and held on tightly.

But the four friends could see the terror in the boys' eyes.

Suddenly, they heard shouts as all the parents and the park ranger arrived. Mr. Coleman and Nick and Pete's dad slid down the steep bank. The park ranger climbed up the tree and pulled the net and the boat toward the shore. Mr. Coleman grabbed the boat and held it steady while Mr. Stuckey helped his sons up the bank.

Everyone cheered as they reached the top . . . except the ranger. He jumped from the tree and marched over to Nick and Pete, hands on his hips and a scowl on his face.

But before he had a chance to speak, Nick and Pete apologized. "We're really sorry," they said.

Then they turned to Mr. Coleman, Mr. Parker, and the Fairfield Friends.

"You were right," Nick said. "Rules need to be obeyed for safety and to avoid punishment."

"And because it's the right thing to do," added Pete.

Everyone walked back down the beach toward their picnic area. On the way, Nick and Pete stopped and read the rules on the sign.

Things to Think About

What rules didn't the Fairfield Friends and Nick and Pete obey? ·

_____

_____

How did the Fairfield Friends and Nick and Pete act after the ranger pointed out the rules?

_____

_____

Because they didn't obey the rules, what might have happened to Nick and Pete?

_____

_____

Read Leviticus 18:4 and 19:37. What does God say about rules and laws?

_____

_____

Read Romans 13:1–5 and Leviticus 25:18. Why else should you obey rules and those in charge?

_____

_____

Read Romans 2:13 and 1 Peter 2:13–14. What happens when you follow rules and obey people in charge?

_____

_____

Let's Act it Out!

Memorize Romans 13:5.

Make a list of the rules you must follow in your house, at your school, and in your community. Why were these rules made? Discuss what might happen if people decide not to follow the rules. Choose one and draw a picture showing the outcome of the broken rule.

_____

_____

_____

_____

2

Ice Water

"Hurry up, Hutch!" yelled Ceely again. She pounded on the bathroom door. "We'll be late for the games!"

"I'll get out when I'm ready to get out!" Hutch shouted back.

Ceely and Hutch and the rest of the Fairfield Friends had planned to meet at the community recreation center. The center held races every two weeks for all the kids in Morgandale. Lots of parents stayed to watch. Ceely and Hutch's grandparents often stopped by to watch, too.

When Hutch finally finished, Ceely quickly stepped into the tub and turned on the shower. As the water hit her back, she jumped. "It's ice cold!" she shrieked. She wrapped her bathrobe around her and stomped into Hutch's room. "You used all the hot water! Now I have to wait for it to heat up again."

Hutch shrugged.

An hour later, the Colemans were finally on their way to the rec center.

"What took you two so long?" asked Mrs. Coleman.

"It's Ceely's fault," growled Hutch. "She waited too long to take her shower."

"No way!" roared Ceely. "You're the one who hogged all the hot water. You're the reason we're late."

"That's enough," said Mr. Coleman.

Hutch stuck out his tongue at Ceely. Ceely made a face back.

"Where have you guys been?!" Roberto asked Ceely and Hutch as they joined the Fairfield Friends in the gym.

"You made us miss the first race," Valerie added.

Ceely and Hutch glared at each other and began their fight all over again.

"Cut it out," Cameron said. "We need to get ready for the second event."

The friends lined up at one end of the gym. When the starter shouted "go," Min raced down the gym floor with a short stick in her hand. As she arrived back at the start, she handed her stick to Hutch.

Hutch, a fast runner, took the lead. He galloped back up the gym. But then he saw that Ceely was next to go. Hutch handed Ceely the stick so hard that she dropped it. It slid across the floor. By the time she got it, the friends were in last place.

"What's wrong with you guys?" Cameron asked angrily.

"You made us lose the race," continued Roberto, frowning.

Next they lined up for the basketball toss. When it was Hutch's turn, he studied the basket. Just as he shot the ball, Ceely yelled out, "Hot water hog!" Hutch jumped. The ball flew to the left and missed the basket. The Fairfield Friends came in last again.

"You two are making us lose every event," Min complained.

"Stop acting like jerks," Roberto added.

"Who are you calling a jerk?" Ceely asked, her voice rising.

The Fairfield Friends began arguing and fighting among themselves now. They couldn't work together as a team at all. They came in last in every event.

"What on earth happened to all of you out there?" asked Roberto's grandpop when the friends joined their parents. Ceely and Hutch's

grandparents, who had arrived in time for the last few events, stood off to one side.

"It looked like Ceely and Hutch were angry when they arrived," said Mr. Hing.

"Well, they should have been able to stop fighting when they got here," Mr. Parker said. He turned to Mr. Coleman. "Perhaps they need some stronger discipline."

"I'll run my family the way I see best," snapped Mr. Coleman.

"They sure weren't acting their best this morning," Mrs. Stevens finished.

After scowling at one another, the parents

and kids turned and walked away.

When the Colemans arrived home, Dad sent Ceely and Hutch to their rooms.

Before long, Grandma and Grandpa Coleman pulled into the driveway. A minute later, Dad called Ceely and Hutch to the family room.

"We saw what happened this morning," said Grandpa.

"So we stopped at the Hosanna Christian Bookstore to get a video," Grandma added.

"We think all of you need to watch it," said Grandpa, popping the video in the VCR.

The story was about two neighbors, Mr. Allen and Mr. Hale. In the fall, leaves from Mr. Allen's maple tree fell into Mr. Hale's yard. Mr. Hale demanded that Mr. Allen rake up the leaves since it was his tree. But Mr. Allen refused. He said the leaves had fallen on Mr. Hale's lawn, so they were his problem.

The argument turned into a huge battle. Soon their children started their own fights at school. It wasn't long until the whole neighborhood took sides with either Mr. Allen or Mr. Hale. Finally, Mr. Hale took Mr. Allen to court. The judge decided that Mr. Allen had to rake the leaves since it was his tree.

That evening, when Mr. Hale took the trash

out, Mr. Allen was waiting for him. He pointed a gun at Mr. Hale and shot him. Mr. Hale died three days later.

At the funeral service, the pastor read Proverbs 17:14. " 'Starting a quarrel is like a leak in a dam. So stop the quarrel before a fight breaks out.' How awful that our selfish and uncaring ways start a silly disagreement," said Pastor Kent. "Like a leak in a dam that grows bigger until it explodes, an argument can become a war with horrible results."

When the movie was over, the Colemans looked at one another. Ceely and her mom had tears in their eyes. Mr. Coleman put his arm around Hutch.

"I think we just learned a very important lesson, didn't we," he said.

Ceely and Hutch nodded.

"We need to make things right with our friends," said Mom.

"I'm on my way," Dad replied as he picked up the phone.

That evening the Hings, the Parkers, Mr. Ruiz, Mrs. Stevens, and the rest of the Fairfield Friends arrived at the Coleman house. First Ceely and Hutch apologized to their friends. Then Mr. and Mrs. Coleman did the same.

"We learned how fast a small disagreement

can build into a war," explained Mr. Coleman, "after we watched a video today."

"Maybe we should all see the video," suggested Mr. Ruiz.

While Mr. Coleman set up the tape, Mrs. Coleman called Charlie's Pizzeria.

After they had finished the video, Cameron, Roberto, Valerie, and Min apologized to one another for getting caught up in the fight. Their parents apologized for the unkind words spoken at the community center. Soon the pizzas arrived, and the room filled with sounds of munching, laughing, and fixed friendships.

––––––––

Two weeks later, the friends met at the rec center again. The first event was a three-legged race. The friends divided into pairs and tied a rope around the two inside legs. Each pair stomped up and down the gym, working together in perfect rhythm. The Fairfield Friends won the race.

During a relay, they passed a ball carefully over their heads to the one behind them. Although Valerie dropped the ball once, the rest of the smooth passes helped them come in second. The Fairfield Friends continued working together as a team without any fighting. They won two more races and came in third in the basketball toss.

"That was a great time," Ceely said as they rode home in their van.

"Sure was," Hutch agreed.

"And we're going to have a super time tonight," added Ceely excitedly.

"I can't wait," said Hutch.

They were planning to spend the night at Jeff and Jenny Noble's, friends of theirs from school. But a phone call from Jenny when the Colemans arrived home ended their plans. Jenny and Jeff had had a big fight, and they couldn't have any friends over for a week.

Ceely and Hutch looked at each other and sighed. Then they plodded slowly upstairs.

"I'm going to take a shower," said Hutch. "I'm sweaty from the races."

"Same here," Ceely said. "I'll take one after you're finished."

Hutch's shower lasted ten minutes. When Ceely got in a short time later, the water was nice and hot.

Things to Think About

How did Ceely and Hutch's fight get started? How did their fight affect others?

_____

_____

What made Ceely and Hutch and their parents work out the problem with the other Fairfield families?

_____

_____

How were Ceely and Hutch affected by someone else's fight?

_____

_____

Read Philippians 2:14–15; 2 Timothy 2:23–24; and James 1:19–20. Why should God's people not fight?

_____

_____

Read Proverbs 17:14. How can you keep a disagreement from turning into a fight?

_____

_____

Read Mark 9:33–35 and James 4:1. What is it that really starts a fight?

_____

_____

Let's Act It Out!

Memorize Proverbs 17:14.

Explain why each of the situations below could lead to a fight. Then come up with ways to avoid the fight.

1. You can't reach the peanut butter in the cupboard, so you ask your older brother to get it for you. He tells you to get it yourself and walks away.

2. A friend promises to ride bikes with you on Saturday. But then she decides to Rollerblade with another friend.

3. Your sister has told you to stay out of her room, but she finds you in it anyway.

4. You brag all day to a friend about winning

first place in a gymnastics meet, knowing that she was cut from the team.

5. You and your brother enter the bathroom at the same time to take showers. Both of you claim to have gotten there first.

6. A classmate trips on the playground at recess. You keep imitating how she fell the rest of the day.

7. A teammate runs up to you after a baseball game and tells you that you've been voted the most valuable player. After you tell your family and friends, the teammate tells you he was just kidding.

8. You've been watching TV for an hour. Your sister says she wants to watch a show now, but you've already started another show and tell her to get lost.

9. You have a friend over to play, and your brother keeps following you around and spying on you.

10. Your sister is on the phone. You keep doing silly things in front of her, copycatting everything she says, and making faces at her.

3

The Mysterious Woman

Roberto again read the verse taped to his mirror. "James 5:15," he began. " 'And the prayer that is said in faith will make the sick person well. The Lord will heal him.' "

Roberto had found the verse by using a concordance, a sort of dictionary to help find verses on a certain topic. He wanted to be sure the Bible said that God heals people.

"Are you ready to go?" Ramone yelled from the living room.

"Yeah, I'm coming," Roberto shouted back. He scooped up Freckles and carried him to his pen outside.

A few minutes later, Ramone and Roberto arrived at the hospital. Ramone had rushed Grandpop to the emergency room the day before after he'd complained of chest pains. The doctor had kept Grandpop overnight to run some tests.

After visiting with Grandpop, the doctor spoke to Roberto and Ramone. "The tests showed that two of the arteries, or tubes, leading out of your grandfather's heart are blocked. I'll perform a small operation tomorrow to clear them so the blood can flow better." Dr. Hoffman paused. "Do either of you have any questions?"

"How long will Grandpop stay in the hospital?" asked Ramone.

"If all goes well with the surgery, he'll be able to go home in a few days," he answered.

———

Three days later, Ramone and Roberto excitedly rode the elevator to the third floor of the hospital to take Grandpop home. But as they passed the nurses' desk, a nurse stopped them.

"You're Mr. Ruiz's grandsons, aren't you?" she asked.

Ramone and Roberto nodded.

"Please wait here a minute. Dr. Hoffman would like to talk to you."

When Dr. Hoffman arrived, he took them to the large visitor's room at the end of the hall.

"I'm sorry," he began. "But your grandpop can't leave the hospital today as planned. He hasn't improved as much as I'd hoped by this time. He's unconscious right now—it's like a very deep sleep. He won't wake up until his brain is ready to wake him up."

"How long will that be?" choked Roberto, tears rolling down his cheeks.

"Roberto, I just don't know," answered Dr. Hoffman. "Hopefully not long."

"Thanks, Doctor," said Ramone. He stared silently out the window. Roberto sobbed softly next to him.

"Let's go to the chapel," Ramone said finally. He put an arm around Roberto and led him toward the door.

Inside the chapel on the first floor, the hospital's minister, or chaplain, greeted them. "I'm Chaplain Walters. Have you been visiting someone in the hospital?"

"Our grandfather," answered Ramone.

"He's really sick," said Roberto. "And I thought God could heal him," he added, sniffing. "But I guess He can't."

"Oh, God has the power to heal anybody," said Chaplain Walters. "If that's what He has planned for that person."

"But what if God chooses not to make

Grandpop well?" cried Roberto. "What if he dies like . . . like . . ."

"Like Mom and Dad?" Ramone asked gently.

Roberto wiped his eyes and nodded.

"Our parents died in a car accident when Roberto was four," Ramone explained to the chaplain. "Grandpop is our only relative."

Chaplain Walters sighed, understanding Roberto's great fear of losing his grandpop, too. "My favorite Bible verse is Romans 8:28," he said. " 'We know that in everything God works for the good of those who love him.' Roberto, things may not turn out how we want them to," he continued. "And we may not know what the 'good' thing is until we reach heaven. But God is in control. He has promised His Christian children that something good will come out of everything, even something terrible."

Chaplain Walters patted Roberto on the shoulder. "God also promises to help us during our troubles," he continued. "Psalm 46:1 says, 'God is our protection and our strength. He always helps in times of trouble.' God will give you the courage to get through this tough time, Roberto, if you ask for His help."

When they got home, Ramone pulled a dish

of macaroni and cheese out of the refrigerator and heated it in the microwave. The ladies' fellowship at church had brought meals for them while Grandpop was in the hospital. After the brothers prayed for Grandpop and asked for courage, Roberto dug into his macaroni. But Ramone pushed his plate away after only a few bites.

Roberto frowned. "Why'd you stop eating?" he asked.

"I'm not really that hungry," Ramone answered.

Later that evening, when Roberto went to bed, Ramone went to bed, too. He told Roberto he was kind of tired.

———

The next morning when Roberto woke up, Ramone was still asleep. *But Ramone has a class at the college at 8:00!* he remembered.

Roberto knocked on Ramone's door and stepped inside. Ramone lay in bed, tossing and turning. Roberto could see sweat all over his body.

"Ramone, what's wrong?!" Roberto cried, running toward the bed.

"I'm having really bad stomach cramps," said Ramone weakly. "I can't even get up. You better call an ambulance. Then call Mrs. Thompson, Grandpop's friend from church, and tell her what happened. You can stay with her until I'm better."

Half an hour later, Mrs. Thompson and Roberto waited in the visitors' room at the hospital. Neither said much. Finally, Mrs. Thompson broke the silence. "Try not to worry," she said to Roberto.

"I'm trying really hard not to," he answered. "I know God will give me the strength to get through this." Roberto picked up a Bible from a table. He turned to Romans 8:28 and told her what he'd learned about the verse.

Mrs. Thompson shared some verses with Roberto, too. While they talked, a woman at the other end of the room kept looking over at them. She strolled around the room several times, acting very mysterious. Finally, she sat down next to Roberto and Mrs. Thompson, opened a magazine, and began to read.

But Roberto noticed she wasn't turning any pages. *She's not reading that magazine,* thought Roberto. *I think she's listening to us!*

Just then a nurse came to take Roberto and Mrs. Thompson to Ramone's room. As they left, Roberto saw the woman put down the magazine and pick up the Bible.

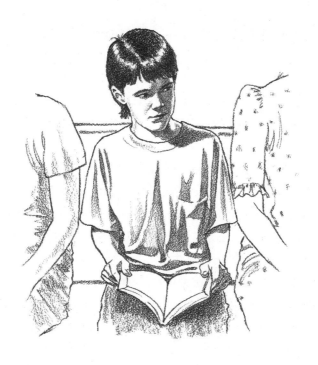

Ramone was still half asleep from the surgery to remove his appendix. It had become infected, explained the nurse. The infection had caused the stomach cramps. But the operation had gone well, and Ramone would be fine in a few days.

After leaving Ramone, Roberto and Mrs. Thompson visited Grandpop. Roberto held Grandpop's hand as he talked to him. He didn't know whether Grandpop could even hear him. But he told him how he learned that God makes good things happen out of bad ones.

Suddenly, Roberto felt a weak squeeze on

his hand. Then another. "Grandpop squeezed my hand!" Roberto shouted.

A nurse called Dr. Hoffman, who checked Grandpop. He reported that he would probably wake up in the next few hours.

Roberto and Mrs. Thompson stayed until visiting hours were over. During the elevator ride to the lobby, they thanked God for healing Ramone and Grandpop. As the elevator door opened, Roberto saw the woman from the visitors' room enter the chapel.

Roberto began to think. *Because of Grandpop's and Ramone's illnesses, Mrs. Thompson and I were here discussing God and quoting Bible verses. That woman was in the visitors' room because someone she loves must be in the hospital, too. And I'm sure she was listening to us.* Roberto watched the chapel door close. *Maybe she's going to ask God for help to get through this time. Maybe she'll become a Christian someday!*

And suddenly, Roberto knew what the "good" was.

Things to Think About

Why was Roberto so worried about Grand-pop?

_____

_____

Why didn't Roberto get as upset over Ramone's sickness as he did when Grandpop had his heart surgery?

_____

_____

What was the "good" thing that came from Grandpop and Ramone being sick?

_____

_____

Read Job 2:9–10; James 1:2–4; and Romans 5:3–4. Who sends trials and hard times? Why are they sent?

_____

_____

Read Ephesians 1:11. Do things always work out the way we want them to? According to whose plans do they work out?

_____

_____

Read Joshua 1:5 and Psalm 46:1. What has God promised us during hard times?

_____

_____

Let's Act It Out!

Memorize Romans 8:28.

Suppose a friend of yours is going through a hard time. What could you say to help your friend understand trials and to have courage during hard times? Now act out the scene.

Using a Bible that has a concordance, look up key words about the Christian life such as forgiveness, trust, hope, love, joy, patience, etc. Now look up some of the verses listed. Choose some favorites, write them down, and memorize them.

_____

_____

_____

_____

4

The Green-Eyed Monster

H ow are things at school?" Valerie's dad asked her as he put two dishes on the table.

Valerie and her little sister, Bonnie, were spending the weekend with their dad. Once Bonnie had settled into bed, Valerie had asked for some ice cream.

"Not too great," answered Valerie, digging her spoon into a mound of chocolate. "My grades in math have been mostly C's," she continued. "I wish I was good in math like Brian or Stacey."

"If you tried your very hardest," said Dad, "then a C is OK."

"And another thing happened," Valerie raced on. "My gym teacher said I'm good in gymnastics. She told me to ask about taking classes at the Morgan Valley Gymnastics Center. Mom said it costs too much. But Rachel Moore started classes there, and she's terrible!" exclaimed Valerie, her face turning pink. She gulped some air.

"Then last week," she continued, her voice rising even more, "we told about our summer vacations. The other kids traveled to really cool places. All I did was go to the seashore!"

"My bunny can't sleep," said a voice. Bonnie stood in the doorway, clutching a stuffed rabbit.

"OK," said Dad as he stood up. "Let's see if we can tell Bunny a bedtime story."

"And Bonnie gets way too much attention," Valerie finished.

Dad returned ten minutes later. "Valerie," he began, "you can't spend your life envying others. People sometimes say envy is a green-eyed monster. It takes over your life, clawing its way deeper into your heart and then all the way to your bones." Dad paused. "Didn't you learn a Bible verse about envy rotting your body or bones or something?"

Valerie shrugged as if she couldn't remember even though Proverbs 14:30 had popped right into her head. *"Peace of mind means a healthy body. But jealousy will rot your bones,"* Valerie said to herself.

"Well, anyway," continued Dad, "you need to be thankful for what you have."

Like what? thought Valerie.

———

After breakfast the next morning, Valerie, Bonnie, and their dad drove to the Jakes' farm. Dad was helping Mr. Jake put up a new fence. Mrs. Jake offered to watch Bonnie. And Valerie could play with Elizabeth, the Jakes' daughter, who was only a year older than she was.

"Your room is really cool," said Valerie as Elizabeth led her into her room. She looked enviously at the white canopy above the bed. She touched the frilly pink curtains at each window, wishing they could be hers.

Elizabeth shrugged. "I'm getting sort of tired of it," she said. "Where do you go to school?" she asked Valerie.

"Fairfield Elementary," she said.

"Do you ride a bus?"

Valerie shook her head. "Nope. The school is only about four blocks from my house. I usually walk or ride my bike there with friends."

"You are so lucky," said Elizabeth. "My bus ride takes almost an hour. And none of my friends live anywhere near me. You can go to the mall, the movies, or the park anytime you want, too. You've got everything, and I'm stuck out here with nothing!" She stopped, panting for breath.

Valerie stared at Elizabeth. She felt like she was looking in a mirror at herself. *I never thought someone would be envious of me!*

"Living in a town is nice," Valerie said. "But it's great here in the country, too."

"Yeah, right," said Elizabeth, sighing.

That afternoon, they hiked in the woods. The only sounds were the crunching leaves under their feet and a few Canada geese honking overhead. Later they rowed a boat all around a pond.

"It's really awesome here," said Valerie as their boat rippled through the water. "There's lots to do." But Elizabeth didn't say a word. *She still isn't happy with what she has,* realized Valerie. *How can I make her understand?* Suddenly, Valerie smiled. She had an idea.

———

The following Friday, Elizabeth arrived at Valerie's house to spend the night. Valerie handed her a sleeping bag and said they'd be sleeping in the family room in the basement. As Elizabeth put her overnight bag down, Valerie saw her frown. The worn brown carpet and old green furniture weren't very nice. Valerie's plan had worked. She was sure Elizabeth already missed her pretty bedroom.

"Hi," said Bonnie shyly, appearing suddenly. "Like my bunny?" she asked.

"Go away, Bonnie," snapped Valerie. "We're busy."

"Oh, come on," said Elizabeth. "Let her stay. I'd much rather have a little sister than two older brothers bossing me around."

That evening, after wriggling into their sleeping bags, they talked awhile. Elizabeth soon fell asleep. Valerie, though, lay awake, thinking about her plans for the next day.

She had told the Fairfield Friends all about her visit and how she learned not to be envious anymore. She explained that Elizabeth was having the same problem. They all agreed to help Elizabeth realize that what she had wasn't so bad after all.

———

The friends met at Valerie's the next morning. They planned to go to the park even though they knew that Saturday mornings were really crowded. They also planned to take the long way to the park. They wanted Elizabeth to see, hear, and smell all the not-so-great things about living in a town. And right before they left, Valerie whispered something to Bonnie and pointed quickly toward the basement.

"I'll bet it's fun living in the country," said Min as they crossed Ridge Street.

"Not really," Elizabeth answered. "It's too quiet and too boring."

Just then a police car and then an ambulance raced by, their sirens screaming. Elizabeth held her ears.

"But you get to go hiking and boating anytime you want," shouted Roberto as they passed a man drilling into the street with a jackhammer. Suddenly, he grabbed Ceely as she started to turn the corner. She had forgotten they were going to the park a different way.

Elizabeth looked at the others. "Isn't there any place around here you can go hiking?" she asked.

"The closest place is Laurel Lake, and that's about twenty-five miles from here," Hutch explained.

All at once the friends began to cough.

Elizabeth rubbed her eyes. They stung and watered. "Where's all this smoke coming from?" she asked.

"The rubber factory is burning stuff," said Cameron. He pointed to a smokestack across the street, belching thick black smoke.

"It's awful," Elizabeth said. They walked for another twenty minutes. "It sure is a long way to the park," she said.

The Fairfield Friends glanced at one another, holding back their smiles.

They finally arrived at the park, only to find

that every piece of equipment was being used. Elizabeth and Ceely waited for their turns on the swings, but other kids kept butting in line. They soon grew tired of the crowd and decided to leave.

After eating lunch at Valerie's, they headed to the basement. Elizabeth reached the bottom step and stopped. Everything that she'd neatly repacked into her bag was now thrown all over the basement.

"Sorry," said Valerie as she helped pick up the things. "Bonnie must have gotten into it. She does stuff like that a lot."

After hanging out and talking for an hour, Elizabeth was bored. "Isn't there anything else to do?" she asked.

"Not really," answered Valerie.

Finally 4:00 came, and Mrs. Jake arrived to pick up Elizabeth. The friends said good-bye to her as she climbed up into the truck. "See ya," she said, waving to them out the window.

As the truck backed out the driveway, Mrs. Jake asked Elizabeth if she'd had a good time. The friends listened closely.

"Yeah," she answered. "But I can't wait to get home."

"Yes!" cheered the friends after the truck drove out of sight. "I think she likes what she has after all," said Valerie.

"What do you want to do now?" Ceely asked the others.

"Let's go back to the park for a while," suggested Valerie. "It won't be crowded now. Besides, we can get there in five minutes if we go the right way."

The Fairfield Friends laughed as they raced each other to the park.

Things to Think About

Who and what were Valerie and Elizabeth envious of?

_____

_____

_____

What happened that helped Valerie stop envying others and learn to appreciate what she has?

_____

_____

_____

What did the Fairfield Friends do to help Elizabeth stop being envious and to enjoy the things she has?

_____

_____

_____

Read Proverbs 14:30; James 3:14;
1 Corinthians 3:3; and Philippians 4:11.
What is the outcome of being envious? What is the outcome of *not* being envious?

_____

_____

Read Deuteronomy 26:11 and 1 Timothy 6:17. What are some of the causes of envy?

_____

_____

_____

Explain how envy "rots the bones."

_____

_____

Let's Act It Out!

Memorize Proverbs 14:30.

Make a "My Life" booklet. Place two or three pieces of paper together and fold in half. Place three staples along the crease. On each page, draw a picture of some of the wonderful things in your life that God has given you.

Figure out the following code for an important thought to remember.

A | B | C   J   N· | O· | P·   W·
D | E | F   M K   Q· | R· | S·   Z· ·X
G | H | I   L   T· | U· | V·   Y·

⅃⌐⌐⎕⌐⌐ ∧⌐⊔⌐⊡ ∧⌐⌐⎕

⊏⌐⊡ ⌐⊓⎕ ∨⅃∧ ⌐⌐ ⌐⊏,

⊏⌐⊡ ⌐⌐⊐ ⊓⅃⊡ ⌐⌐⌐⎕⊿

∧⌐⌐ >⌐⌐⊓.

The answer is on page 125.

5

Lost Mountain

Mr. Parker braked gently as he rounded the sharp turn in the narrow mountain road. Suddenly, the van slid sideways on some ice right toward the road's edge.

"Aaaah!" rose a group cry.

"Hang in there, everyone," said Mr. Parker. "We're almost to the top."

It was Christmas vacation, and the Fairfield Friends were attending the yearly youth retreat held by Cameron's church. The friends looked forward to the three days of fun and learning about God. They also looked forward to the scary drive up the mountain to be over.

After arriving at Lost Mountain Ski Resort, the kids settled into the two rooms of cabin 6. Then they hurried to the lodge to join the rest in one of the meeting rooms.

"Welcome, everyone," said Pastor Millen, the youth pastor at Cameron's church. "And an extra big welcome to all our guests."

"The theme of our retreat this year is 'worship,'" continued Pastor Clark, an assistant pastor. "Hebrews 12:28 says that Christians are to 'worship God in a way that pleases Him' and do so 'with respect.' Over the next couple days, each cabin will work on a project so we can learn what kind of worship pleases God."

By the time he'd explained the projects, it was lunchtime. The group ate together in the large dining room along with other guests at the lodge. That afternoon, the kids played in the snow, sledding and building snowmen. Finally, everyone gathered for the annual Lost Mountain snowball fight. After a hard-fought battle, Pastor Millen declared the team made up of cabins 1, 2, and 3 as the winners.

———

The next morning, the Fairfield Friends hiked across the field to the lodge for breakfast. "What project should we work on?" Valerie asked the others. She scooped up a bit of snow with her mitten and took a bite.

"Didn't one of the pastors say a group

would plan a whole worship service?" Min
asked.

"That would be awesome," said Hutch.

"Let's vote on it," suggested Ceely. All six
agreed on the church worship project.

"OK, everyone. Listen up," called Pastor
Clark as the friends found seats in the meeting
room after breakfast. "It's time to decide who's
doing what project. Who'd like to work on a
booklet showing different ways we can worship
God?"

The kids in cabin 2 jumped to their feet.

Pastor Millen handed them a sheet of guide-lines to follow.

Next, cabin 1 chose to work on a play show-ing both the wrong way and the right way to act during the church service.

"Now," continued Pastor Clark, "who wants to plan our worship service?"

The Fairfield Friends leaped from their chairs before he even finished his sentence. Soon they sat huddled at a table, discussing Sunday's service.

"We should have a choir sing," suggested Roberto.

"Or a children's sermon," Valerie added.

"Maybe there could be a report on mission-aries," said Min.

"And even a skit," finished Hutch.

The friends looked from one to another si-lently. Although they all attended different kinds of churches in Morgandale, they never realized how different their services were.

"We never have a children's sermon," said Min. "All the kids stay and listen to the regular sermon."

"And who ever heard of doing a skit?" asked Cameron.

"Well, the skit could be a story from the Bible," argued Ceely.

"But what's wrong with a choir?" Roberto asked.

"Nothing," said Valerie. "My church has a children's choir, adult choir, and a bell choir. Sometimes they all perform in the service."

"But there has to be enough time for the sermon," said Cameron. "It's the most important part."

"The pastor at my church always gets fifteen to twenty minutes," Roberto said.

"At my church," said Min, "Pastor Tran preaches for thirty or forty minutes."

"Forty minutes?!" the others exclaimed.

"Whoa! What's all the ruckus over here?" asked Pastor Clark as he sat down with them.

"We can't decide on how our worship service should be," explained Cameron.

Pastor Clark nodded. "It's hard sometimes because everybody has different ideas. Why don't you pretend you are starting a new church," he suggested. "And the only guide you have for worship is God's words in the Bible. Let me get you those verses we looked up yesterday."

The Fairfield Friends opened their Bibles first to Psalm 69:30. " 'I will praise God in a song. I will honor him by giving thanks,' " read Min.

"First Timothy 4:13," began Roberto. " '... devote yourself to the public reading of Scripture, to preaching and to teaching' " (NIV).

Cameron cleared his throat. "Matthew 15:8–9. 'These people show honor to me with words. But their hearts are far from me. Their worship of me is worthless. The things they teach are nothing but human rules they have memorized.' "

" 'Honor the Lord by giving him part of your wealth. . . . ' Proverbs 3:9," finished Valerie.

The friends looked at one another. According to these Scriptures, it was clear that a worship service needed to include singing, praying, Bible reading, and an offering. But preaching and teaching were the most important parts, and worship should come from the heart. Reciting poems together or mumbling memorized prayers would not be pleasing to God. With these things in mind, the Fairfield Friends spent the rest of the day planning the worship service.

———

The next morning, the friends set up chairs in the meeting room. They also met with the other kids they had asked to be part of the service. At 10:00 Min began to play some hymns on the piano. Just as they were ready to start the service, the group watched two families come in and sit down.

After they found seats, Min began to play. Everyone rose and sang "Holy, Holy, Holy." Pastor Millen offered a prayer then, praising and thanking God for all His blessings. He also asked for health to be restored to the sick and for the forgiveness of sins.

The Scripture reading followed. Pastor Millen told the congregation to read along in their Bibles as he read 1 John 1:4–6. Pastor Clark's sermon would focus on those verses later.

Next came the offering. Two boys passed baskets up and down the rows of chairs. During the offering, the kids from cabin 4 walked to the front of the room and sang "O Worship the King." They had learned the hymn as part of their project on worshiping God in song.

After presenting the offering to God and singing another hymn, Pastor Clark began his sermon. "I've been preaching straight through the book of First John at our church," he began. "It's a good way to explain what the verses really mean so they can help us in our lives as Christians."

When Pastor Clark finished his sermon, everyone rose for the final hymn. Afterward, the two families introduced themselves to the Fairfield Friends and the pastors.

"We heard the music," explained Mrs. Grove. "And since we're churchgoers, we decided to join the service."

"We're very glad you did," Pastor Millen responded.

"And what a wonderful service it was," said Mrs. Hoke. "For the first time, I felt like I was worshiping from the heart."

"Same here," added her husband, Fred.

"And I even understood some of the things that Pastor Clark talked about," said their six-year-old son, Nathan.

Mr. Grove looked at all the Fairfield Friends. "This service helped me realize that the purpose of worship is not to entertain the people. . . ."

"But to allow people the chance to honor and worship God," finished Mr. Hoke.

That afternoon, as Mr. Parker drove the friends back to Morgandale, they told him all about their worship service. Then they chatted excitedly about next year's retreat, the project they would work on . . . and who would win the big snowball fight.

Things to Think About

What did the Fairfield Friends disagree about while planning the worship service?

_____

_____

_____

After reading the Bible verses, what was their church service like?

_____

_____

_____

Who benefited from the service and why?

_____

_____

_____

Read Hebrews 12:28; John 4:23; and the NIV of Matthew 15:8. What kind of worship pleases God? What does not please Him?

_____

_____

_____

Read Proverbs 3:9; Nehemiah 9:3; Psalm
69:30; and the NIV of 1 Timothy 4:13. What
should be included in the worship service?

_____

_____

_____

What is the main purpose of the church
service?

_____

_____

_____

Let's Act It Out!

Memorize Hebrews 12:28.

Plan your own worship service. Write a para-
graph describing what you would include.

_____

_____

_____

_____

A Fairfield Friends Devotional Adventure

Find these words about worship hidden up, down, across, backward, and diagonally in the letter box below.

thanksgiving   preaching   offering
prayer   honor   respect
scripture   praise   singing
heartfelt   teaching   confession

S	A	B	N	Q	P	Z	P	N	S	R	N
F	R	E	S	P	E	C	T	C	E	A	O
D	K	L	I	X	V	J	M	Y	H	I	I
G	H	O	N	O	R	C	A	P	V	Z	S
N	H	M	G	J	N	R	K	R	P	C	S
O	G	R	I	F	P	D	E	A	R	Q	G
F	C	O	N	F	E	S	S	I	O	N	N
F	P	T	G	I	W	O	P	S	N	B	I
E	T	H	E	A	R	T	F	E	L	T	H
R	U	Y	W	X	U	R	S	C	Q	Y	C
I	O	L	M	R	S	B	V	R	X	A	A
N	P	R	E	A	C	H	I	N	G	Z	E
G	N	I	V	I	G	S	K	N	A	H	T

Answer is on page 125.

6

Lemons and Grapes

Cameron aimed at the basket and shot. "Yes!" he shouted as the ball slid through the net.

"It's not over yet, bro'," said Philip. He charged in for a lay-up. He missed!

Cameron leaped to catch the rebound. As he landed on the driveway, his foot twisted. Cameron fell hard onto his right side with his arm under him. The sound of a stick breaking crackled through the air. Only it wasn't a stick; it was Cameron's arm.

Two hours later, Cameron returned from the hospital. His right arm and hand had a hard white cast on it. Not only had he broken his arm but his wrist, too.

At supper, Cameron had to eat with his left hand. Every time he tried to scoop up some peas with his spoon, they rolled away or fell off. Justine, who had been watching, burst out laughing.

"It's not funny," roared Cameron. "This is horrible," he continued. "I can't do anything. I can't eat. I can't write. How am I supposed to wash my hair? I can't even use my compu—" Cameron froze. "Oh no," he groaned. "If I can't type, I can't be in the math competition."

Each year the best math students from the local schools met in a computer room in the high school. On each student's computer screen, math problems appeared one at a time. Each student had to work the problem and then type in his answer.

"And I had a really good shot at winning this year," grumbled Cameron.

———

After school the next day, Cameron sat in the kitchen eating a cookie. Finishing the milk in his glass, he slammed it back onto the table.

"Cameron," said his mom, who was preparing dinner, "I don't need the glasses broken."

"Sorry," mumbled Cameron. He continued to stare at the table, his lower lip sticking out.

"Are you planning to sit there and mope until your arm heals?" Mom asked.

"There isn't anything else I can do," answered Cameron.

His mom looked at the empty milk jug. "Well, since you finished the last of the milk, maybe you could walk to the Ready Mart and get some more."

"Do I have to?" Cameron asked.

Mom sighed. "Your arm is broken, Cameron, not your leg."

After buying the milk, Cameron headed home. But he took a different way. As he started up Juniper Street, he noticed the "For Sale" sign no longer sat in the yard at 337.

While he looked at the house, the door flew open. A lady in a wheelchair wheeled through the doorway and down a ramp where the steps had been. The chair rolled all by itself.

Cool, thought Cameron. *An electric wheelchair.* He watched her get her mail and roll back up the ramp. But then her chair got stuck in the doorway.

"Here, let me help," said Cameron, running across the yard and up the ramp. He wriggled a magazine from under the wheel and handed it to the lady.

The woman laughed loudly. "So that's what was holding me up!" she exclaimed. She turned to Cameron. "Well, aren't you the brave one. You came to rescue me when you aren't even in one piece yourself. C'mon in," she said. "Tell me how you broke your bones."

Cameron followed her into the living room. She said her name was Miss Cooper and that she'd moved in last week. Then Cameron introduced himself and told her about his arm and the math contest.

"That sure is a bummer," she said, shaking her head. "I'd go nuts, too, if I couldn't use my computer."

"You have a computer?" Cameron asked.

Miss Cooper winked at him. "Follow me," she answered, chuckling.

When Cameron entered the room at the end of the hall, he stopped and stared. Miss Cooper's two computers, screens, and printers filled one whole side of the room.

"Awesome! exclaimed Cameron, his eyes wide and shiny. "I've never seen such great computer stuff."

Cameron looked at the rest of the room.

The other walls were covered from the middle on down with cross-stitch and needlepoint pieces. Each one had a Bible verse on it. After Cameron read some, he stared at Miss Cooper.

Miss Cooper smiled. "I'll bet you're wondering why all the verses are about being joyful, especially if I'm in this wheelchair."

Cameron nodded.

Miss Cooper explained. "When I was ten, I dove into a pool and hit my head on the bottom. I've been unable to move from the waist down ever since."

"But, but . . . why are you so happy and joyful?" Cameron blurted out.

"I wasn't when it first happened, Cameron. I envied my friends who could do all the things I couldn't. I moped around, doing nothing. But then I came across a Bible verse one day." She pointed to a needlepoint on the wall. "First Thessalonians 5:16. 'Be joyful always' (NIV). I realized, then, that God wants us to be joyful no matter what our problems. I also decided to make grape juice."

"Huh?" asked Cameron.

Miss Cooper grinned again. "I wanted to make lemonade," she began. "But when God sent me grapes instead of lemons, I simply made grape juice. In other words, when God took one thing away, I just decided to use something else He'd given me.

"So in college I came up with a program that allows me to create my own needlepoints on the computer. I send the designs to craft stores all over the country. But first I always do the needlepoint to make sure it looks right. It's turned into a nice career. God has been really good to me."

As Cameron walked home, lemons and grapes swirled through his head. *If I can't be in the math contest, I guess I'll work on my Civil War project for history class instead.*

After supper, Cameron searched for clothes that he could use to pretend to be a slave, a soldier, and Abraham Lincoln. He wanted to share their different views about the Civil War. When he was dressed as each one, he asked Philip to film him with the video camera.

———

The next day, Justine and Cameron walked to the Ready Mart. Cameron needed notebook paper, Justine wanted some candy, and Mom needed bananas.

While strolling up Oak Drive on their way back home, they suddenly heard loud, angry barking. Cameron and Justine turned around and saw a huge black dog charging right at them!

Justine screamed and began to run. Cameron froze, staring at the dog's sharp teeth as it ran toward him. Just as the dog leaped at him, Cameron stuck out his arm. Strong jaws clamped onto his cast. The dog bit and chewed. But Cameron held him off.

Finally, the dog's owner ran over to them. "I'm so sorry," said the man. He led the dog into the house and then returned to Cameron and Justine. "I just bought him and didn't re-

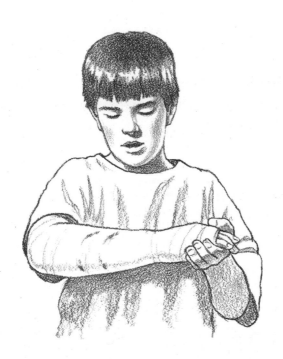

alize he could push up the latch on the gate. Are you hurt?"

Cameron checked himself. "I'm OK."

The man looked at Cameron's cast. Large teeth dents covered it. "I'll bet you're the first person ever to be happy with a broken arm," he said.

———

A few days later, Cameron visited Miss Cooper. He had gotten an A on his history project and wanted to show her the video. He also wanted to tell her about the dog attack. After Cameron showed her his cast, he turned on the VCR. Then they settled back to watch his video, each holding a glass of grape juice.

Things to Think About

Why was Cameron joyless and unhappy?

_____

_____

How did he find joy and regain a good attitude?

_____

_____

How did his cast help him?

_____

_____

Read Galatians 5:22–23. Where does joy come from?

_____

_____

Read Psalm 90:14 and 1 Thessalonians 5:16. When and how often should you be joyful?

_____

_____

Read Habbakuk 3:17–19; Romans 15:13; and Colossians 1:10–12. How can you remain joyful when things don't go right?

_____

_____

Explain what Miss Cooper meant when she said, "I wanted to make lemonade. But when God sent me grapes instead of lemons, I simply made grape juice."

_____

_____

Let's Act It Out!

Memorize 1 Thessalonians 5:16.

Proverbs 15:30 says, "A cheerful look brings joy to the heart . . ." (NIV). Draw a picture of yourself showing a "cheerful look."

Make a "joy" magnet for the refrigerator. Cut a piece of construction paper or thin cardboard into a three-inch by two-inch rectangle. Using markers or crayons, make a simple "joyful" design. You could write the word joy in several colors or draw a smile, for example. Cut a three-inch by two-inch piece from a sheet of magnet board (found in hobby and craft stores or in full-service print shops). Glue your design onto the magnet piece. Put your magnet on the refrigerator door to remind you to be joyful always.

7

Tattoo, Dog Collar, Orange Spikes, and Nose Ring

Wow!" shouted Cameron.

"What a shot!" exclaimed Hutch.

"Burke's really on tonight," Roberto said.

The three boys, along with their dads and grandpop, had traveled across the state to watch a professional basketball game.

Suddenly, Burke stole the ball. He turned and drove in for a lay-up. But as he did, he knocked another player onto the floor. The referee blew his whistle and called a charging foul on Burke.

Lennie Burke threw up his hands and stomped over to the referee. Burke yelled in his face, but the referee refused to change his decision.

And then Lennie shoved him. The crowd fell silent. Touching the referee meant Lennie was out of the game. Lennie and the referee stared at each other. Finally, Lennie stormed down the sideline and out of the arena.

"What a jerk!" Cameron said.

"Why didn't he just admit he charged?" asked Roberto.

Grandpop looked at the boys. "Some people insist that they're never wrong, that they never sin. But First John 1:8 says, 'If we say that we have no sin, we are fooling ourselves, and the truth is not in us.' "

A couple days later, the boys watched the sports report on TV at Roberto's house. They were waiting for Ramone to drive them to Charlie's Pizzeria for their free pizza. Every month, kids who read three library books received coupons for free items from local businesses.

"Look at that!" Hutch said suddenly. On the screen was a picture of Lennie Burke.

"Two days ago, Lennie Burke was thrown out of a game," said the announcer, "for pushing a referee." The TV picture returned to a studio where two men sat in chairs. "With me right now is the team spokesman, Mr. Hart, who has a statement to read from Mr. Burke."

Mr. Hart turned toward the camera and began to read. " 'I, Lennie Burke, am sorry that the other player was in my way when I went in for the lay-up. But I did not charge him. I still believe the referee made a bad call. I also apologize to my teammates. If I'd been in the game, we would have won. And a special apology to all my fans who weren't able to see me play.' "

"Unbelievable!" exclaimed Cameron. "He still won't admit that he was wrong."

"That was no apology, either," said Hutch.

"He keeps on blaming others even though he is responsible for his own actions," added Ramone as he walked into the room.

"Yeah," agreed Roberto. "No one made him push the ref."

Ten minutes later, they arrived at Charlie's. It was packed.

"Are you guys sure you want to stay?" asked Ramone. "It may take a while to get your pizza."

"I don't think I'll mind waiting for free pizza," said Cameron.

"I wouldn't mind waiting for free anything," Hutch added.

Ramone laughed and turned to leave. As he did, he waved to the employee behind the counter. "Hey, Ross," he yelled. "I'll see you at the meeting tonight."

Ross glanced up from cutting a pizza and waved back.

Ramone looked back at the boys. "I'll be here at 7:00, OK?"

The boys nodded and then started their search for seats. But the only three seats together were at a table where some older boys were already sitting. One had his nose pierced. Another had his hair formed into stiff orange spikes. A skinny one wore a leather dog collar around his neck. The last one had a tattoo of a snake . . . on his forehead.

They stared at the older boys and then at one another.

"They look kind of rough," Roberto said.

"Maybe," said Cameron. "But who cares? I just want to get my pizza."

After putting their jackets on the chairs, they placed their orders. When they returned, they said a quick "hi" to the other guys at the table.

Roberto, Hutch, and Cameron munched on pizza. Between bites, they talked quietly among themselves. All at once, loud laughter exploded from the other end of the table. The three of them watched as the boy with the tattoo pointed to a large piece of yellow cardboard on the wall.

" 'I confess my guilt. I am troubled by my sin. Psalm 38:18,' " read Tattoo.

The boys laughed and pounded the table.

"I took some money from my mom's wallet this morning," said Nose Ring. "But I don't feel guilty. I feel rich!"

Cameron, Hutch, and Roberto glanced briefly at one another. They knew that Charlie Fodder, the owner of the shop, was a Christian.

Putting Bible verses on the wall was Charlie's way of telling others about God.

"Hey!" yelled Dog Collar. "You three down there. Don't you think those signs are funny and stupid?"

"Or are you goody-goody Christians?" Orange Spikes asked.

"Um . . . uh . . . no . . ." Cameron stammered.

"They're really funny," added Hutch.

"Well, you aren't laughing," said Dog Collar.

The boys forced a chuckle.

"What does that one say behind you?" Nose Ring asked.

Cameron turned around and began to read. " 'Love your neighbor as you love yourself.' "

"Well, I love myself a lot," said Tattoo. "I guess that means I can give lots of lovin' to Megan, who sits next to me in English class."

The boys howled and made loud kissing sounds at one another. Cameron, Hutch, and Roberto laughed along, too.

After they read and laughed at some more verses, the older boys left, leaving all their trash on the table. The employee walked over and began to clean it up. "Aren't you Ramone's brother?" he asked Roberto as he threw cups in a trash can nearby.

"Yeah," he answered. "How'd you know?"

"I saw you come in with him. We both belong to the Students for Christ group at the college. In fact, we have a meeting tonight. My name's Ross." He paused while dumping plates in the can. "You know," he continued, "I was shocked that you laughed along with those guys at the table."

"We didn't want to," said Roberto. "But they made us."

"What do you mean, they made you? It was your choice whether you did or not."

"But they started it," protested Cameron.

"Yeah," Hutch agreed. "We didn't really do anything."

Ross sat down at the table. "You sinned because you pretended you didn't know God." He turned to a sign on the back wall and read, " 'If anyone is ashamed of me and my teaching, then I will be ashamed of him. Luke 9:26.' " Ross went on. "You continue to sin because you won't admit to your sinful actions. I hate to say it, but you're acting like Lennie Burke, that basketball player who won't admit to his charging foul."

Cameron, Hutch, and Roberto looked at

one another. Their eyes widened and their mouths fell open as the awful truth sank in.

While the boys waited outside for Ramone, each bowed his head and asked God to forgive him of his sin. A horn beeped when they had finished.

After they piled inside the truck, Ramone looked at them, smiling slightly. "Either you guys were counting the cracks in the sidewalk or praying."

The boys laughed.

"So what's wrong?" asked Ramone.

"You'll hear all about it tonight from Ross," said Roberto.

As they drove home, they listened to the radio. When the sports came on, they heard the latest on Lennie Burke. He'd gotten mad at a newspaper reporter and punched him. Lennie Burke was off the team for the rest of the season.

Things to Think About

What were Lennie Burke's sins?

_____

_____

_____

What sins did Cameron, Hutch, and Roberto commit?

_____

_____

_____

How did they feel after Ross showed them the Bible verse and told them they were acting like Lennie Burke? What did they do about it?

_____

_____

_____

Read Acts 3:19; Psalm 32:5; 38:18; and 1 John 1:8–9. Who should you admit your guilt and repent of your sins to? Why?

_____

_____

_____

Read Luke 9:26 and Philippians 1:28. Why should you not be afraid to stand up for God?

_____

_____

_____

Read Mark 14:66–72. What was Peter's sin? How did he feel after realizing his sin?

_____

_____

_____

Let's Act It Out!

Memorize 1 John 1:8.

Look up each of the following Bible verses one at a time. Match the verse to one of the following situations that deals with a particular sin. Write down the verse as well as the sin that has been committed.

Blaze on Rocky Ridge

Colossians 3:13

Proverbs 11:24

1 John 2:15

1 Thessalonians 5:17

Proverbs 12:22

Hebrews 13:16

Proverbs 17:14

Ephesians 6:1

1 Corinthians 6:8

Proverbs 14:30

James 1:26

James 4:16

1. Mandy, a girl at school, is wearing a new outfit. You really wish you could have an outfit like that. You also wish your hair was as pretty as Carly's. And you'd give anything to be able to sing as well as Sally.

2. You won an art contest, and you keep telling everyone how good an artist you are.

3. Your parents tell you that you can't go to Steve's house. But while you're visiting Joe, your friends decide to go to Steve's. You go along since your parents won't know about it.

4. You don't feel like doing your homework. At school the next day, you tell your teacher you'd been sick all last evening and couldn't do it.

5. You're playing a card game with a friend. When she leaves to go to the bathroom, you look at her cards so you can win.

6. Your brother accidentally bumps into you, causing you to drop and break a glass of milk. You yell at him, calling him a "stupid, clumsy moron with the body of a whale and a brain filled with worms."

7. Your Sunday school class has decided to earn money for the homeless shelter by doing chores at home. You earn $7.75. Before you enter your class, you stick the three quarters in your pocket. You figure you should get to keep some of the money since you did all the work.

8. You tell your sister that you know something she doesn't just to bug her. When she demands to know what it is, you tell her you forgot what it is. She gets mad and shoves you. You pinch her on the arm.

9. Your best friend forgot your birthday. Even though she's apologized, you refuse to talk to her.

---

10. There's one piece of chocolate cake left, and you and your brother both want it. When you get off the school bus, you race each other into the house. Since you got to the cake first, you eat the whole piece.

---

11. Your grandma died last year even though you asked God every day to make her well. Now your grandfather is sick. But since God didn't help before, you aren't going to waste time asking for His help now.

---

12. The kids at school all listen to some really cool music and watch all the popular shows on TV. You know some of the songs have bad words in them, and you've heard the shows sometimes make fun of Christians. But you really want to fit in with everybody. So you buy the music and watch the shows.

Answers are on page 125–126.

Copy the prayer of repentance below onto a recipe card. Keep it in a place you will see it each day, like on your dresser or taped to your mirror. Each day fill in the blanks as you ask God's forgiveness. Add more blanks if you need to.

> Dear God,
> I come to you now to tell you my sins and to ask for your forgiveness. I'm sorry for _____ and for _____ and for _____. I know _____ and _____ and _____ are wrong. Please forgive me and help me to do what's right. Amen.

8

Lights in the Night

Good morning, everyone. I'm Miss Morgan. Welcome to Vacation Bible School. This week we're going to learn how our un-Christian actions hurt others. Let's divide into groups now, and you can begin talking about today's subject—breaking promises to others."

Hutch and Valerie joined four other kids at a table. They picked up the work sheet Miss Morgan had passed out and began to read.

"Hey, everybody," whispered Dereck, one of the boys at their table. "Have I ever got a story for you guys. You know Scott Young over there?" he asked, pointing with his head toward another table.

Valerie nodded, but Hutch didn't.

"He goes to Fairfield Elementary," Valerie explained. "He only came in April, and he's really quiet. None of us knows him very well."

"So tell us what happened," said Kate eagerly.

"Well," began Dereck. "Yesterday I saw a police car pull into his driveway. He was inside for a long time."

"Wow," said Evan. "I wonder who did what?"

"I'll bet his older brother, Dave, got into trouble," suggested Ruth. "He's in high school with my sister. She said a neighbor of her best friend's cousin said he was kind of weird."

The others nodded in agreement.

"I wonder what he did?" asked Hutch.

"Maybe something terrible," Valerie suggested.

"In that case, we better stay away from him," said Dereck.

"And we better tell the other kids about him, too," added Kate.

After the other kids in the class heard about Scott, they all decided to stay away from him. While choosing up sides for kickball at playtime, no one picked Scott. When they lined up to go in, everyone pushed Scott to the end of the line. Scott looked at them, sadness lining his face.

———

The next day, as Valerie and Hutch joined their table, they noticed that Dereck was so excited he could barely sit still.

"I'm glad you're finally here," he said to them. "You won't believe what happened! Yesterday afternoon on my way to the pool, I saw Scott's brother and his dad get into a police car!"

"His dad?!" exclaimed Hutch.

Dereck nodded.

"Wow," said Evan. "Maybe the whole family did something."

"Maybe they even robbed a house," added Ruth.

At snack time, Kate passed out the cookies her mom had sent along. Kate served everyone two big cookies. But she picked out smaller ones for Scott, both of them broken. And during the rest of the morning, the kids said mean things to Scott, just loud enough for him to hear.

"Robber," said Ruth as she passed him on her way to the water fountain.

"Thief, thief, stole some beef," sang Dereck softly when they lined up to go outside.

"What did you steal?" Valerie asked when she ran past him to catch a Frisbee.

When class ended and they got ready to

leave, they all looked at Scott. He had tears in his eyes.

"Serves him right," Dereck said while watching Scott wipe his eyes, "for what he and his family did."

That evening, Valerie and Hutch walked to the park to watch a softball game. When it was over, they strolled home, talking and enjoying the pink and orange sunset.

Suddenly, Hutch stopped. "Did you see that?" he asked Valerie.

"See what?" Valerie wondered.

"That light in the trees in that backyard

over there," answered Hutch, pointing.

Valerie searched the tree-darkened yard with her eyes. "I see it," she said. "And you know what? Scott's family lives just two doors down from there."

Hutch's eyes widened. "I'll bet it's the Youngs sneaking around in the yard. Do you think . . . I mean, maybe they're—"

"Going to break in and rob those houses?" said Valerie, finishing Hutch's thought.

Hutch nodded. "We should call the police."

"But where?" asked Valerie. "If we wait till we get home, they might be gone."

Hutch looked around him. "C'mon," he said. "Roberto's friend Mrs. Thompson lives in the next block. We can call from there."

After they told Mrs. Thompson about the lights in the yard, they dialed the police and gave the address. Then Hutch and Valerie hurried back to Elm Street.

They stood on the other side of the road, watching from behind a high hedge. A police car drove slowly down the street and then stopped. A policeman slid from his car and turned on a big flashlight.

All at once he shouted, "Halt! This is the police!" He reached inside the car window and turned on the siren and the lights.

Doors flew open, and the neighbors on the block bolted out of their homes and toward the police car. Valerie and Hutch quickly crossed the street to see what was happening. They stood behind a large group of neighbors in the dark shadow of a pine tree. "Look," whispered Hutch. "It's them."

They watched as Scott, Dave, and their dad ran out from behind a house. "What's the problem?" Scott's dad asked.

"Oh . . . Mr. Young . . . hello," said the police officer. "It's Officer Keen. I took you to the police station yesterday."

"Sure. I remember," said Mr. Young, nodding. "What's wrong?"

"The station got a call a few minutes ago about some people sneaking around in the backyards with a flashlight."

"That was us," said Dave. "We just got a cat. We left her out this afternoon, and she hasn't come back yet."

"We thought maybe she got stuck in a tree," added Scott.

Out of the shadows slinked a furry body. It meowed as it trotted across the lawn.

"Case solved," said Officer Keen as Scott scooped up the cat. "By the way," he said, turning to Dave. "We jailed the man you saw robbing Martin's Market. Describing what he looked like when I was here the other day really helped. It wasn't long before one of our officers found him. But going to the police station with me yesterday and making sure he was the right man allowed us to arrest him."

Valerie and Hutch looked at each other, their mouths hanging open. Dave had seen a robbery, and because of him, the robber had been caught and put in jail.

———

The next day at Vacation Bible School, Miss Morgan told the class that the day's subject was gossip and rumors. "Gossip," she explained, "is worthless, empty talk about others. A rumor is a story someone tells without knowing whether it's true or not. And as Proverbs 18:8 tells us, 'The words of a gossip are like tasty bits of food. People take them all in.' "

As the kids pulled their chairs into one big circle to discuss the topic, Hutch and Valerie whispered to those in their group. They explained how they'd been totally wrong about Scott and his family. The other kids shrugged to show they didn't care.

But during recess, Valerie and Hutch told Scott what had happened and apologized to him. They thought Scott would be mad, but he started to laugh.

"How silly," Scott said. "How could anybody build a whole story like that out of one little thing?"

Hutch and Valerie looked at each other and laughed, too.

After gathering in their groups again, Miss Morgan gave directions for the day's craft project. While the kids at Valerie and Hutch's table cut pictures from magazines, Ruth began gossiping about Miss Morgan. "I saw her talking to some guy in the parking lot this morning. Maybe it's her boyfriend."

"Hey," said Kate. "Maybe she's getting married."

"C'mon, guys," said Hutch. "Don't start another rumor. He might have been just a friend or even her brother."

"Remember what happened with Scott?" Valerie asked.

But the kids kept on gossiping, so Valerie and Hutch ignored them. After class, they stopped Scott on their way out. And that evening, the three met at the park to watch a softball game.

Things to Think About

What rumor about Scott and his family did the kids start and then gossip about?

_____

_____

What was the truth about the Young family?

_____

_____

How did the rumors hurt Scott?

_____

_____

Read Proverbs 10:8–10. What happens to someone who gossips?

_____

_____

Read Ecclesiates 7:25 and Proverbs 26:20. How can gossip and untrue stories be stopped?

_____

_____

Read John 21:20–23. How did Jesus' own disciples gossip?

_____

_____

Let's Act It Out!

Memorize Proverbs 18:8.

Make a list of ways that rumors get started.

_____

_____

Play the game Birds on a Wire. While standing in a line, the first person whispers a sentence or two in the ear of the person standing next to him. That person repeats what he heard (or thinks he heard) to the next person, and so on. The last person in the line has to say out loud what he heard. Was the final story the same as the first? Probably not.

Tip: For a larger group (eight or more), two or three sentences are enough for the message; for smaller groups, make the message a little longer or tell a short story.

9

Good News for Africa

O h, thank you, Mother," said Min excitedly. "I'm going to call Ceely right now."

Min was so glad her mother had given permission for Ceely to spend the night. Since she had no brothers or sisters, having lots of sleepovers with a friend was the next best thing.

"Ceely?" asked Min after she answered the phone. "My mother said you can spend the night. Ask your mom if it's OK." Min tapped her foot on the floor while she waited for Ceely to return. "You can? Fantastic!" exclaimed Min. "Bring along that new glow-in-the-dark nail polish you got and all your hair stuff. We can do each other's hair while we watch a video."

After planning some more activities, they

agreed to meet at the Morgandale Community Pool for the afternoon.

Later, when Min arrived home from swimming, she practiced the piano and quickly did her chores. She was eager to get to her room and set things up for Ceely. Her dad had already opened the foldaway cot. Min only needed to put the sheets on.

While she tugged the pillowcase onto the pillow, she heard the phone ring. A short time later, Mother knocked on her door.

"Min," said Mother gently. "That was Pastor Tran on the phone. He asked if we could have a missionary couple spend the weekend with us. They had planned to stay with the Shoemakers, but Mrs. Shoemaker got sick this morning. I told him we could put the missionaries in your bedroom. You can sleep in Grandmother's room in your sleeping bag."

"But, Mother!" cried Min. "Ceely is coming. We planned to paint our nails and watch a video and everything!"

"I know, honey, and I'm sorry," Mother said as she stroked Min's shiny hair. "But sometimes we must do things that we don't like. Ceely can come another time."

Min frowned. She knew arguing would do no good. After walking slowly down the stairs and flopping onto the couch, she called Ceely.

An hour later Min was in her room and heard the doorbell ring. A few minutes later her door opened.

"Min, this is Mr. and Mrs. Stuart," said Mother. "They're taking a month-long break from their missionary duties in Africa. They'll be visiting several churches in the United States who, like our church, help support their work."

"Hello," said Min softly.

"Min," said Mr. Stuart, "we understand that we've made you call off a sleepover tonight. We're very sorry."

"It's OK," Min said politely.

"There's a verse in Hebrews 13," continued Mr. Stuart. "I think it's verse 16. It says, 'Do not forget to do good to others. And share with them what you have. These are the sacrifices that please God.' It was really good of you to share your room with us, Min."

"Especially knowing the sacrifice you made," added Mrs. Stuart.

Min smiled. *I didn't think that giving up my room was some kind of a good deed*, thought Min. *Or that God would be pleased with it.*

At supper, Min chatted more than usual. She felt so proud of her good deed.

Later on she called Ceely. "Why don't you come to church with me on Sunday," asked Min. "After lunch we can hang out in my room. The Stuarts only need to sleep there. They won't mind if we use the room for a while. Besides, they know what a good deed I did by giving up my plans and sharing my room."

On Sunday morning, while dressing for church in the bathroom, Min discovered she had forgotten her slip. She knocked lightly on her door. "Mr. and Mrs. Stuart?" she called. "I need to get something out of my room."

"Sure, Min. Come on in," called Mr. Stuart.

When Min opened the door, she stared at her room. Papers and booklets lay on the floor, her bed, the cot, and her desk.

Mrs. Stuart saw Min's shocked face and explained. "Part of the reason for our visit in the United States is to allow us to stock up on supplies. These papers are all part of the Gospel packet we give out. We have five hundred booklets and papers to staple together. We thought we'd get started on them this afternoon."

Min tried to say something, but her voice wouldn't work. She simply nodded. After she opened her dresser drawer and found her slip, she quickly left her room.

When the Hings arrived at church, Ceely ran over to Min. "My parents just dropped me off," she said. "I can't wait until this afternoon."

Min sighed loudly. "We can't use my room this afternoon. The Stuarts have papers and stuff all over my bedroom."

"Can't they move them?" Ceely asked.

"I couldn't ask," Min said. "They expect me to keep on doing good deeds since I shared my room. I wonder how much more I have to give up?"

An hour later, at the beginning of the church service, Pastor Tran welcomed the Stuarts. Then he quoted a Bible verse. "Hebrews 13:16," he said.

As he began to read, Min jumped slightly. *That's the same verse the Stuarts quoted to me.*

When Pastor Tran finished reading, he spoke to the congregation. "The Stuarts clearly show what this verse is about. The good works they do with the African people are truly amazing. They've given out almost five hundred Gospel packets to share the Good News of Jesus Christ with those who don't know Him. And they make unbelievable sacrifices to do so. The hut-like house they live in doesn't even have running water."

Min couldn't believe what she heard. She looked at the floor and studied the pattern in the carpet. *And I thought what I did was so great,* she thought.

During dinner at the Hings', Grandmother Hing asked the Stuarts to tell about their missionary work. Min listened closely as they told about rains that turned the dirt roads into a sticky swamp of mud. Their house had been broken into many times by people who didn't want them there. And enormous mosquitoes buzzed everywhere in huge masses like thick black smoke.

"It does get difficult sometimes," said Mrs. Stuart.

"But," continued Mr. Stuart, "when another person finally understands what we're teaching and becomes a Christian . . . well . . . the unpleasant things don't seem very important." He paused, heaved a sigh, then pushed his chair away from the table. "Well, dear," he said, turning to his wife. "We better get to those Gospel tracts."

While Min and Ceely cleared the table, they talked softly to each other. Then they quietly slipped up the stairs and walked slowly toward

Min's room. They stopped at the door and peeked inside. On the floor sat Mr. and Mrs. Stuart, a stapler in front of each of them.

Mr. Stuart looked up and smiled. "Hi, Min, Ceely. Sorry about your room again, Min. I'm afraid we've been a bit of a problem for you."

"Oh, not at all," Min said. "In fact, we wanted to see if we could help you with the Gospel tracts."

"You're on," answered Mr. Stuart. "I'm getting too old to sit scrunched up on the floor." He stood up and stretched his back.

"Help sounds good to me, too," said Mrs.

Stuart, laughing. "I've pounded so many sta-ples that my hand is getting a blister on it."

Min and Ceely took their places on the floor. Ceely gathered the papers, and Min sta-pled them together. They added the packet to the pile of finished ones. As they began an-other, they asked the Stuarts to tell more about their mission to spread the Good News of Christ in Africa.

Things to Think About

What good deeds did Min and the Stuarts do?

_____

_____

How did Min come to realize she had been prideful about her good works?

_____

_____

What good deed did Min and Ceely eventually end up doing?

_____

_____

Read Ephesians 6:8; James 3:13; Colossians 3:17, 23; and Titus 3:8. Why and how should you perform good deeds?

_____

_____

Read Matthew 6:1–4. What are "loud" and "silent" good works?

_____

_____

Read 1 Peter 2:20; 2 Thessalonians 2:16; and Galations 6:9. How are missionaries able to do their work for the Lord, even when they suffer?

_____

_____

Let's Act It Out!

Memorize 1 Timothy 6:18.

Learn about the missionaries your church supports. Who are they, what country are they serving in, what successes and problems are they having? Write down these facts on recipe cards, one for each missionary, so you can pray for one every day.

Write letters to missionaries, encouraging them in their work. Perhaps you could include a small gift of something that they cannot get where they are.

Perform a "silent" good deed this week. Try to do one every week.

10

Blaze on Rocky Ridge

Hurry up, everybody," Hutch called softly. "There's a hawk sitting in a tree up here."

The other Fairfield Friends, Mr. and Mrs. Coleman, Ramone, and his friend Ross walked swiftly and silently up the trail. Up in a tree sat a beautiful brown and white hawk perched like a king on a throne. They passed around the binoculars, or magnifying glasses, to get a closer look.

"Can you believe God made such a beautiful bird?" asked Mr. Coleman after the group had carefully slipped away so they wouldn't startle the hawk.

"And how about those cardinals and blue jays?" Mrs. Coleman added. "What a paint box of reds and blues God had when He created them."

The group was on a two-day hike in Pine Grove State Forest. They'd spent the day hiking on Rocky Ridge searching for birds, bugs, flowers, and animals.

"What's that white flower?" Valerie asked. "It almost looks like lace."

Cameron, who had the wild flower guide, thumbed through the pages. "Here it is," he said. "It's called Queen Anne's lace."

"How did God make all this stuff?" Ceely asked.

"We'll never understand how He did it," answered Mr. Coleman. "But we can be sure that He is the one who did the creating."

"In fact," Ramone added, "the very first verse in the Bible, Genesis 1:1, says, 'In the beginning, God created the sky and the earth.'"

"Genesis 1 also tells us in verse 26 that God planned for man to rule over the fish, the birds, and over all the animals and plants on earth," Ross added.

"So we are responsible for protecting and caring for everything on God's earth," explained Mr. Coleman.

A short time later, the group arrived at their campsite. Mrs. Coleman unpacked the food. The Fairfield Friends gathered wood so Mr. Coleman could build a fire.

While they watched him, he explained that the fire had to be built inside the circle of rocks in their campsite. Called a fire ring, it kept the flames from spreading. He also told them to keep a close watch on the fire. Since there hadn't been much rain lately, a single spark could land in the dry grass and start a forest fire.

Later on, Ramone, Ross, and the Fairfield Friends laid out ground covers and sleeping bags.

"I hear music," said Ramone.

"Me too," said Cameron and Ceely at the same time.

"Great," said Ramone, sounding frustrated. "Just what we need in God's peaceful mountains—rock music."

"Let's go ask them to turn it down a bit," suggested Ross.

A few minutes later, the music stopped. But it was another ten minutes before Ramone and Ross returned.

"What took you guys so long?" Roberto asked.

Ramone began to explain. "Two teenage boys, Ryan and Dan, are camped at the next site a short way up the trail. We caught them throwing rocks at a bird in a tree."

"We shouted to them to stop," Ross continued. "But they couldn't hear us over the music. Finally, they turned it down."

"We started to leave, but we noticed there was no fire ring. When we asked them where it was, they pointed to a bunch of rocks sitting all over the ground."

"And you'll never guess what they had used them for," Ross said. "They told us they dropped each stone on a spider or a daddy longlegs."

"Oh, gross," said Min. Hutch and Valerie wrinkled their faces.

"We reminded them about how dry it is and not to build a fire until they put the rocks back," added Ramone.

"Did they put them back?" asked Cameron.

"They started to and said they'd do the rest," Ross answered. "So we headed back. We were getting hungry."

Just as Ross finished speaking, Mr. Coleman shouted it was time for dinner. Each camper roasted a hot dog over the fire on a stick. Later, they toasted marshmallows and sang songs around the fire. After prayers, they finally crawled into their sleeping bags, tired from their long day.

———

The next morning, the hikers strapped on their backpacks and started down the path to Horse Tail Falls. An hour later they stopped to rest. Mrs. Coleman looked for birds with the binoculars. "What's all that fog over there?" she asked her husband.

Mr. Coleman looked through the binoculars. "That's no fog," he said. "It's smoke! There must be a forest fire!"

"What do we do now?!" Ceely asked worriedly as she, Valerie, and Min huddled around Mrs. Coleman.

"First we need to know which way the fire is moving so we don't run into it," said Mr. Coleman. "Hutch, think you can climb up that tree?"

"Sure, Dad," he answered.

Once lifted onto the first branch, Hutch quickly climbed up the branches. "There is a fire . . . a pretty big one . . . back near our campsite, I think." He paused. "Hey!" he yelled. "I see two guys. They're trapped! The fire is between them and the trail!"

Ramone and Ross looked at each other, knowing it was Ryan and Dan. "We have to help them!" Ross said.

"Let's go!" shouted Ramone, already running toward the teenage boys.

The Fairfield Friends and Mr. and Mrs. Coleman continued quickly along the trail, away from the fire. Every few seconds one of them turned around to see if Ramone and Ross and Ryan and Dan were coming.

Suddenly, the wind picked up. The fire turned right toward the friends. As the smoke got thicker, they began to cough.

Cameron looked behind them. He wiped his eyes. "I see them!" he yelled. "They're coming." The group waited for the four to catch up.

Just then a huge pine tree only a few hundred feet away caught fire. The kids screamed

as it blazed skyward like a lighted torch! And then the wind shifted again, turning the fire away from them.

An hour later, they reached Horse Tail Falls. They rested briefly and thanked God for their safety. After filling their canteens with water, they picked up the main trail. In half an hour, they arrived at the ranger station.

"Ranger Shank spotted the flames from the fire tower," explained Ranger Riley. "I sent some men out to your campsites. But you'd all left, and the men didn't know which way you'd gone. Glad you made it out safely, though."

A voice on the radio interrupted him. It was Ranger Shank reporting that the fire had spread out of control. "We also know where the fire started," he continued. "We found a campsite without a fire ring."

All eyes turned to look at Dan and Ryan.

Just then a soft, low sound like a rolling bowling ball filled the air.

"Did you hear that?" Min asked.

"I did," said Mrs. Coleman.

"Me too," Roberto agreed.

"It sounded like—" began Ceely.

"Thunder!" they all cried together.

Within minutes, heavy rain poured down. Half an hour later Ranger Shank called in again. The rain had put out most of the flames, and the men had the fire under control.

"How much of the ridge burned?" Ranger Riley asked.

"About 150 acres," Ranger Shank answered. "It's completely burned out. The trees are gone, the wild flowers, the birds, and all the animals. I don't think you could even find a daddy long-legs out there."

"We're sorry," burst out Ryan. "It was our fault."

"We didn't put the rocks back," Dan said to Ross and Ramone. "But we'll do whatever it takes to bring the forest back."

Two weeks later, they proved true to their word. An ad in the *Morgandale Daily Sentinel* asked people to help plant new trees on Rocky Ridge.

That Saturday, the Fairfield Friends met at the Pine Grove ranger station along with hundreds of other volunteers. Rows and rows of pine saplings only a foot high stood all around. Ranger Riley told the friends that Ryan and Dan had bought all three hundred trees themselves.

After everyone had picked up a tree or a

shovel, the volunteers started off. But the ones in the lead soon stopped, not sure of which trail to take. Ryan and Dan saw Roberto, Min, Ceely, Hutch, Valerie, and Cameron in the crowd and yelled to them. Then, after moving to the front of the group, the Fairfield Friends led the way to Rocky Ridge.

Things to Think About

Did Ryan and Dan care about God's world? How do you know?

_____

_____

What happened that helped them learn to value and care for God's world?

_____

_____

What did Ryan and Dan, the Fairfield Friends, and others volunteer to do?

_____

_____

Read Genesis 1:1–22; Psalm 148:1–12; 74:17; 89:11–12a. List all the things God created or is in control of.

_____

_____

Read Isaiah 43:7 and Psalm 135:6 (NIV). Why did God create the world and everything in it?

_____

_____

Let's Act It Out!

Memorize Genesis 1:1.

Make a mural on seven pieces of paper taped together, each piece standing for one day. Following Genesis 1:1–2:3, draw pictures showing what God created on each day. For the seventh day, you can simply write "God Rested."

Choose an outdoor place in God's world—one that you and your family or group enjoy—to draw. After the background is drawn, take turns adding to the picture by drawing something found in that area. For example, you could draw a field and then add flowers, trees, butterflies, and bugs.

Answers

CHAPTER FOUR

Accept your life for the way it is, for God has given you much.

CHAPTER FIVE

```
S   A   B   N   Q   P   Z   P   N   S   R   N
F   R   E   S   P   E   C   T   C   E   A   O
D   K   L   I   X   V   J   M   Y   H   I   I
G   H   O   N   O   R   C   A   P   V   Z   S
N   H   M   G   J   N   R   K   R   P   C   S
O   G   R   I   F   P   D   E   A   R   Q   G
F   C   O   N   F   E   S   S   I   O   N   N
F   P   T   G   I   W   O   P   S   N   B   I
E   T   H   E   A   R   T   F   E   L   T   H
R   U   Y   W   X   U   R   S   C   Q   Y   C
I   O   L   M   R   S   B   V   R   X   A   A
N   P   R   E   A   C   H   I   N   G   Z   E
G   N   I   V   I   G   S   K   N   A   H   T
```

CHAPTER SEVEN

1. Proverbs 14:30—envying others
2. James 4:16—bragging
3. Ephesians 6:1—disobeying parents
4. Proverbs 12:22—lying
5. 1 Corinthians 6:8—cheating

6. James 1:26—not controlling your tongue
7. Proverbs 11:24—not giving what you should
8. Proverbs 17:14—fighting
9. Colossians 3:13—not forgiving others
10. Hebrews 13:16—not sharing
11. 1 Thessalonians 5:17—not praying
12. 1 John 2:15—loving the world more than you love God